ELIANA AND
DAWSON
HUSSEY

To an Angel
Ellen

Cinderella

Retold and illustrated by
Toby Bluth

Adapted from
Charles Perrault

Ideals Publishing Corp.
Nashville, Tennessee

Copyright© MCMLXXXVI by Toby Bluth
All rights reserved. Printed and bound in U.S.A.
Published simultaneously in Canada.

ISBN 0-8249-8152-9

ONCE UPON A TIME, in a kingdom far away, there lived a lovely maiden named Ella. She had a sweet and gentle nature and always went about her chores with a song and a smile.

Ella lived with her cruel stepmother and two ugly stepsisters. Her stepmother forced Ella to work as a maid for the family, doing all of the cooking and cleaning. Her stepsisters were meanspirited, and they taunted Ella about the rags she was forced to wear

while they were dressed in fine gowns.
　　But beautiful clothes could not hide their nasty natures and rags could not hide Ella's gentle grace. Through all of her hardships, she remained pleasant and kind.

Ella's stepmother and stepsisters were jealous of her beauty and sweet disposition, so she was made to sleep in the attic and she was not allowed friends or company.

Ella had a secret hideaway. It was her own little corner by the fireplace. In the evenings, she would sit there warming herself by the cinders and dreaming.

There her imagination could take wings and she could be anywhere or anyone she wanted to be. In her dreams, she might dance through a meadow of flowers or be a great singer, loved and admired by all. Why, she was even free to imagine herself a fairy princess.

Once when Ella emerged from her hideaway, covered with ashes from the cinderbox, her stepfamily ridiculed her, calling her Cinder-Ella. Forever after, that was the only name by which she was called.

Cinderella lived in a kingdom ruled by an old king who lived in a huge castle which towered over the village. The king had a son who would one day become ruler of the kingdom. Now he wanted his son to start taking on some of the responsibilities of ruling the kingdom. Most of all, he wanted to see his son married and with a family.

One day the king called his son to him and said, "My boy, I think it is time for you to get married."

"But, Father," said the prince, "I have not yet found anyone whom I wish to marry."

"I know," said the king, "and I think it is time for you to start looking."

"In time, I will," answered the prince.

But the old king had already made up his mind. "As your father," he said, "and as king," he added for absolute authority, "I have decided that now is the time. We shall give a royal ball to which every unmarried young lady in the kingdom will be invited. There you will select your future bride."

The prince tried to object, but the king would hear none of it. So the prince slouched down, pulling his crown to a disrespectful angle, which annoyed his father all the more.

"The announcement shall be made today," thundered the king. "Now sit up and straighten your crown."

And with that, he stormed off, leaving the prince alone.

The prince had always believed he would fall in love before he married, but that did not look possible now. He felt miserable. He may have been the prince, but at that moment, he felt more like a prisoner.

When Cinderella's stepsisters received their invitations to the ball, they immediately put her to work sewing new gowns, fixing their hair in the latest fashions, curling, starching, and ironing. One sister chose to be dressed all in gold, while the other chose silver. But neither gold nor silver could transform ugliness into beauty.

As Cinderella readied them for the ball, they taunted her, "It's a shame you can't go to the ball, Cinderella. One look at you in your rags and the prince would surely fall in love with one of us," they said sarcastically. And they giggled with high squeals.

And so it went until the night of the ball. As the sun went down and the evening star rose in the sky, Cinderella's stepmother and stepsisters, dressed in all their finery, set off for the ball in their family carriage, convinced that the prince would choose one of them for his bride.

Never in her life had Cinderella felt so sad and all alone. She went to her corner by the fireplace, but this time there were no flights of fancy, no dreams of becoming a fairy princess. There was only a tired and lonely girl with no place to go. And for the first time, Cinderella wept.

Then a strange and marvelous thing happened. The fireplace began to glow with a beautiful blue light that grew brighter and brighter until it filled the entire room. And there, standing in the middle of the light was a sweet, little old lady with a wand in her hand.

Cinderella dried her tears. "Why, who are you?" she asked.

The little old lady smiled. "Child," she said, "I'm your fairy godmother, and I've come to help you. You're going to the ball tonight."

"Going to the ball?" questioned Cinderella. "Why I have no way to get there and I have nothing to wear."

The kind old lady laughed. "These are simple matters for a fairy godmother," she said. "Now, come with me."

And with that, she took Cinderella by the hand and led her into the garden.

"First you must bring me a pumpkin— golden and perfectly formed," said the fairy godmother.

This Cinderella did at once, although she didn't understand what possible use a pumpkin could be.

"Next, I will need six white mice and a rat with very fine whiskers," said the fairy godmother.

Cinderella gathered up the mice and a rat and placed them by the pumpkin.

"Finally, I will need a sleek, green lizard," said the fairy godmother as she bent down to pick up a lizard scurrying across the ground and placed it by the rat.

The fairy godmother waved her magic wand over the pumpkin. It began to glow, and to grow—bigger and bigger until, right before Cinderella's eyes, the pumpkin was transformed into a magnificent coach fit for a princess.

With another wave of the wand, the six

white mice became six white horses, prancing into place before the pumpkin coach.

Again the fairy godmother waved her wand, and this time the rat was turned into a coachman with a very fine mustache. Finally, the lizard became a footman ready to help Cinderella into her coach.

Cinderella was delighted. She laughed and clapped her hands each time the magic occurred. The fairy godmother had one last bit of magic to perform. She lifted her wand and said, "Now, a gown fit for a princess."

Moonbeams and a cloud of mist swirled around Cinderella transforming her rags into a beautiful gown of ruffles and lace. Ribbons and rosebuds magically appeared about the gown. Cinderella whirled around as if she were waltzing, and the lovely dress left behind a shimmering trail of stardust. Looking down, Cinderella saw on her feet two tiny glass slippers.

She had never seen anything so beautiful in all her life. "Oh, godmother," she exclaimed, "how can I ever thank you?"

"There is one thing you must remember," said her fairy godmother.

"What is that?" asked Cinderella.

"You must return before the final stroke of midnight, for at that time, everything will change back to what it was—the carriage, the horses, the coachman, the footman, and even your lovely gown."

"Oh, I will," promised Cinderella.

Then the fairy godmother kissed Cinderella good-bye and vanished as quickly as she had appeared.

The sleek footman helped Cinderella into her coach.

The coachman snapped his whip and the six white horses bolted into action. The magic coach sped through the empty villages, across the open countryside, and onward to the great castle. It moved so fast, the wheels barely touched the cobblestones.

Cinderella was both frightened and excited. In her life, she had known much hard work and sorrow. Now, at least for one magical evening, she could live a dream come true.

Inside the ballroom, the evening had been long for the prince. He had met and danced with many lovely ladies, but none whom he wished for his bride. The king was losing patience with his son and was hiding his temper less and less. As his father's anger mounted, the prince became more defiant. He pulled down his crown to an annoying angle and waited for his father to comment on it. The king was quite vexed.

The two stepsisters had just presented themselves to the prince when Cinderella entered the ballroom. The prince saw her in the distance. He squared his shoulders, raised himself to his full height, and straightened his crown.

The room grew quiet as the prince slowly crossed the floor. The prince stopped, looked into her eyes, and bowed low.

"May I have this dance?" he asked.

Cinderella took his hand and, with his arm about her waist, they began to dance.

Other couples joined in until the ballroom was aglow with lovely ladies and handsome gentlemen in a swirl of color.

In every corner guests whispered, "Who is she?" and "Isn't she beautiful?" No one, including her stepmother and stepsisters, recognized the maiden as Cinderella.

The old king smiled with satisfaction as the prince and Cinderella waltzed out of the ballroom and into the garden. On and on they waltzed in the moonlight. They lost track of everyone and everything, including time. Then Cinderella heard the clock strike twelve.

BONG! BONG! BONG! sounded the gong in the clock tower.

"Oh no!" cried Cinderella, "it's midnight. I must go now."

Before the prince could stop her, Cinderella was running away.

BONG! BONG! BONG!

Cinderella dashed out of the ballroom.

"Wait," the prince shouted, following her.

BONG! BONG! BONG!

Lightning ripped through the sky and rain began to fall.

BONG! BONG! BONG! On the last stroke of twelve, six mice, a rat, and a lizard scurried past a pumpkin in the castle courtyard as a frightened maiden dressed in rags disappeared into the black of night.

The prince stood in the pouring rain looking all about. There was no trace of Cinderella anywhere. What only a minute ago had been a wonderful evening, had quite suddenly turned into confusion. The prince was in despair. Was he never to see her again?

He didn't understand what had happened. He was sure she had felt the same love for him that he had felt for her. Why had she suddenly run away and where was she now, he wondered.

Just then he noticed something on the castle steps. It was a slipper made of glass sparkling in the rain.

The prince picked up the slipper and stared at it for a very long time. He knew that it could belong to no one else but the maiden with whom he had been dancing.

"I will find the lady whose foot fits this slipper," he vowed, "and I will marry her."

The prince told his father of his plan to search the entire kingdom until he found the young lady whose foot would fit the glass slipper.

"But," said the king with concern, "that slipper might fit any number of maidens."

"No," said the prince, "I believe it will fit only the maiden who is its rightful owner. I will find her, Father, and I will marry her."

The king bid his son a sad farewell as the boy set off on his quest.

Throughout the fall, as others celebrated the harvest, the prince searched for his lovely lady. Every lady in the kingdom was allowed to try on the slipper, but alas, it fit none of them.

Winter turned bitter cold, and while others kept warm and secure inside their homes, the determined prince searched on.

He visited every home in the village and every house in the outlying countryside, but still the slipper fit no one. Although he saw many lovely young ladies, none of them were the maiden for whom he searched, and so he went on.

Finally, in the spring, the prince arrived at the home of Cinderella's stepmother and stepsisters. The two girls fluttered about the prince, each claiming to be the owner of the slipper. They argued over who should try on the slipper first. Then the prince saw a young lady doing her chores. He recognized her at once.

The prince walked past the arguing sisters. He walked past their mother. He walked straight to Cinderella.

When she saw the prince coming toward her, Cinderella was embarrassed for she was wearing only rags and looked like a

poor servant girl. But that was not what the prince saw. He saw the lovely lady whom he wanted to make his bride.

The prince kissed Cinderella and then put the glass slipper on her foot. It fit perfectly.

The prince put Cinderella on his horse and they rode off to the castle where they were soon to be married. And they lived happily ever after.